This book belongs to:

_ _ _ _ _ _ _ _

For Nigel, my husband. With love. X
K.S.

Sir Charlie Stinky Socks would like to donate 10% of the royalties from the sale of this book to Naomi House Children's Hospice.

EGMONT
We bring stories to life

First published in Great Britain in 2014
by Egmont UK Limited
The Yellow Building, 1 Nicholas Road, London W11 4AN
www.egmont.co.uk

Text and illustrations copyright © Kristina Stephenson 2014

Kristina Stephenson has asserted her moral rights.

ISBN (HB) 978 14052 6809 7
ISBN (PB) 978 14052 6810 3

A CIP catalogue record for this book is available from the British Library.

THE PIRATE'S CURSE

Kristina Stephenson

EGMONT

Once up on a time

there was a bottle bobbing,
out in the **big**
blue
sea . . .

a sea filled with **pirates** and *magical mermaids*.

Oh, and a **MAN-EATING MONSTER**!

The bottle went on bobbing for six long years
without any sign of stopping.

More's the pity, for inside this bottle
was a worrying little word . . .

HELP!

Shiver me timbers!

Splice the mainsail!

Someone was in trouble.

Oh my!

But never fear,

because land was near, and so was . . .

. . . a bold, brave knight!

Sir Charlie Stinky Socks,
his faithful cat, Envelope, and his good grey mare,
spotted the bottle bobbing in the water.

So they waded out to fetch it.

Splish-
splash

splish-
splash

splish-
splash

Splosh!

"By jinkies!" said Sir Charlie, studying the note. "Someone at sea needs our help. Come on, my faithful, fearless friends, we need to find a ship."

And quicker than you could say, 'Watch out for **pirates**', they headed for adventure.

As luck would have it,
down in the harbour,
a ship was about to set sail.

A motley crew was raising the
gang plank and the captain
was holding the helm.

Thump!

No one noticed the knight and his friends
as the ship sailed out to sea,

until a westerly wind
whipped up
a storm and . . .

blew the
trio's cover.

"For I am Sir Charlie Stinky Socks and my stockings have a **mighty power**.

And consider my cat; not one rat will bother you while *he's* here.

As for my horse;
my horse is, of course . . .

terribly good at . . .

ummm . . .

cleaning!"

Huh?

"If you let us stay," said Sir Charlie to the captain, "think how useful we'll be."

Lucky for the trio the **hairy-scary captain** was surprisingly quick to agree.

The wind grew stronger, thunder roared, but Sir Charlie
went on with his mission.
He was searching for someone
who needed his help;
whoever that someone might be.

Over the sea.
Whooshity-whoosh!

Crash!

Bash!

Smash!

The waves tossed the boat,
which *tipped* and dipped towards . . .

the **rugged rocks**.

Oh my!

Could a pair of socks
save them now?

No!

But something *magical* might.

Time for a knight to use
those socks to do a spot of . . .

"Why else would his motley crew never see him after the sun goes down? He must be more terrifying than the **MAN-EATING MONSTER** when he's locked in his cabin at night.

This **hairy-scary pirate captain** with

a purple patch
on one eye, and . . .

a **picture of his ship**,
the Black Toenail,
painted on his . . ."

"**MONSTER** ahoy!" came the cry from the crow's-nest, and everyone turned to see . . .

the munching, crunching **MAN-EATING MONSTER**, licking his loathsome lips.

"Heavens to Betsy!
We're doomed!" cried the crew.

So, six years ago I
in a bottle and se
hoping that some
come and help me

And that's where
Sir Charlie stepped in.

A fog of flour f

The captain wa

"I don't like bei
he said.
"I li

"... I'm getting pretty good."

Wow!

But – dear oh dear –
no **MAN-EATING MONSTER**
would ever be scared
of *this* **pirate**.

"Not to worry!" said
Sir Charlie to the captain,
"*I've* got a better idea.

You MUST tell the crew what it is you do.
Then get them to fire up the cannons."

. . . he went on eating cake
from **Ye Olde Black Toenail** —

the captain's cake shop,
beside the **big** blue sea.

THE END